W9-CZA-248

Put Beginning Readers on the Right Track with
ALL ABOARD READING™

The All Aboard Reading series is especially designed for beginning readers. Written by noted authors and illustrated in full color, these are books that children really want to read—books to excite their imagination, expand their interests, make them laugh, and support their feelings. With fiction and nonfiction stories that are high interest and curriculum-related, All Aboard Reading books offer something for every young reader. And with four different reading levels, the All Aboard Reading series lets you choose which books are most appropriate for your children and their growing abilities.

Picture Readers
Picture Readers have super-simple texts, with many nouns appearing as rebus pictures. At the end of each book are 24 flash cards—on one side is a rebus picture; on the other side is the written-out word.

Station Stop 1
Station Stop 1 books are best for children who have just begun to read. Simple words and big type make these early reading experiences more comfortable. Picture clues help children to figure out the words on the page. Lots of repetition throughout the text helps children to predict the next word or phrase—an essential step in developing word recognition.

Station Stop 2
Station Stop 2 books are written specifically for children who are reading with help. Short sentences make it easier for early readers to understand what they are reading. Simple plots and simple dialogue help children with reading comprehension.

Station Stop 3
Station Stop 3 books are perfect for children who are reading alone. With longer text and harder words, these books appeal to children who have mastered basic reading skills. More complex stories captivate children who are ready for more challenging books.

In addition to All Aboard Reading books, look for All Aboard Math Readers™ (fiction stories that teach math concepts children are learning in school) and All Aboard Science Readers™ (nonfiction books that explore the most fascinating science topics in age-appropriate language).

All Aboard for happy reading!

Library of Congress Cataloging-in-Publication Data

Mason, Jane.
    Hello, two-wheeler! / by Jane Mason ; illustrated by David Monteith.
       p.   cm.—(All aboard reading)
       Summary: Even though he loves to ride his bicycle, a young boy makes excuses not to because he is the only one of his friends to still have training wheels.
       [1. Bicycles and bicycling—Fiction.] I. Monteith, David, ill. II. Title. III. Series.
    PZ7.M4116He   1995
    [E]—dc20   94-28633
                                                                                                             CIP
ISBN 0-448-40853-8   H I J   AC

HELLO, Two-Wheeler!

By Jane B. Mason
Illustrated by David Monteith

Grosset & Dunlap • New York

It is summer.

And it is hot.

I am hanging around

with my dog Fred.

Outside all the kids zoom
up and down the street
on their two-wheelers.
They yell and have fun.

5

"Why don't you get
your bike out too?"
my mom asks.

6

"No," I say.

"I want to play with Fred."

But that is not really true.

I do not want the kids

to see my training wheels.

I used to love riding my bike

with all the kids.

I liked the feel of the wind.

I liked the blur of the trees.

I liked tooting my bike horn.

But now everybody can ride
without training wheels.
Everybody but you-know-who!

Every night Dad tries to help me.

We go to a big parking lot.

We take off the training wheels.

"Okay," Dad says.

"I will hold on to you.

You just pedal."

So I do.

But then Dad says,

"I am letting go now."

And I get scared.

I think about falling.

My feet won't stay

on the pedals.

And I stop.

It happens every time.

"You can do it,"

Dad keeps saying.

"Just don't think about it."

But how do I do that?

We always end up going home
with my training wheels
back on my bike.

Now the doorbell is ringing.

It is Nicky.

"Do you want to play ball?"

he asks me.

The ball field is far away.
You have to ride your
bike there.
"Sorry," I tell him.
"I have to
clean my room."

17

Later the phone rings.

It is Nate.

"Want to bike down

the big hill?" he asks me.

I think fast.

I fake a sneeze.

ACHOO!

"I can't," I say.

"I have a cold."

Then we hang up.

I am bored.

So I go over to see Tommy.

Tommy lives next door.

At Tommy's house
there are lots of things to do—
without riding a bike.

We work on a model plane.

We play video games.

We shoot hoops.

I am having fun.

Who cares about two-wheelers?

But then our friend Josh
rides by.
"A bunch of kids are going
swimming at the pond.
Want to come?"

Tommy's eyes light up.

But mine do not.

What can I say this time?

"Um. I—I have to wash my dog.

There is a big dog show

coming up."

"It's not until next week,"

Josh says.

"I know." I try to sound cool.

"But I want to get Fred

super clean."

Tommy comes over to me.

"Come on," he says.

"No one will care about
your training wheels."

Tommy is the only one
who knows my secret.

I shake my head.

"You go. Maybe I'll come later."

At home

I flop on the couch.

Fred <u>is</u> kind of smelly.

But I do not want

to give him a bath.

I want to be with my friends

at the pond.

Then I get an idea.

A good idea!

I put on my swim trunks.

I get Dad's tools.

"I am going to the pond,"

I tell my mom.

I hop on my bike and go.

It feels so good to ride!

I like the wind in my face.

I like the blur of the trees.

I like tooting my bike horn.

Soon I am near the pond.

I stop.

I take off my training wheels
and hide them.

Then I walk my bike over

to the kids.

"Hi!" says Tommy.

He looks surprised and happy.

"I'm glad you came."

The kids are swimming.

I jump in.

"Don't you have a cold?"

Nate says.

I say, "It went away.

It must have been

the two-hour kind."

"Did you get Fred washed?"

Josh asks.

I shake my head.

"Nope. We were out of

dog shampoo."

Then somebody starts a water fight.

Nobody asks me anything else.

We have a great time.

But then it is time to go.

We all get on our bikes.

"Oh! Something is not right

with my pedal," I say.

"Lucky for me I have my tools.

You guys go on.

I will catch up."

Tommy gives me a funny look.

But he rides off with the kids.

I walk my bike to the bushes.

I put my training wheels back on.

Then I get on my bike and go.

Nobody will see me now.

They are too far ahead.

I ride past the pond.

I ride down the hill.

I make a turn.

Oh, no! Up ahead

I see all the kids.

Tommy starts shouting.

He is pointing at my wheels.

Oh, no! Oh, no!

Everyone will see.

"Way to go!" Tommy shouts.

What is he talking about?

I look down.

Yikes!

No training wheels.

I keep going.

I am too scared to stop.

I do what Dad says.

I try not to think about it.

I just keep riding.

"See you!" I shout

to the kids.

And do you know what?

I make it all the way home.

Good-bye, training wheels!

Hello, two-wheeler!